Tilly's Big Moment

TC CARNER, MD

Paperback-Press
an imprint of A & S Publishing
A & S Holmes, Inc.

ISBN: 978-1-945669-49-1

CHAPTER 1

The little parachutes of thistledown drifted gracefully past, one suddenly diving downward and tickling the little bunny's nose. She giggled, watching it until it finally wafted out of sight. "Why is everything the way it is, Mr. Brambles? I mean, why do we *have* to die?" the tiny bunny queried her silvered companion.

"I suppose it's apropos," sighed the ancient Rabbit, "since I will be leaving soon, that you've asked me perhaps the most difficult of all questions, Tilly. Not all questions have answers, by the way. I believe somewhere, sometime long ago, I may have known *the* answer to that question, but I'm not so sure any more.

The longer my teeth grow, the more answers to every question there seem to be. I suppose if I had to pick one answer, though, it would be that things,

1

generally speaking, are the way they are because they *can be* that way, Tilly. For example, we can only see a mother Kangaroo with her young Joey in that strange pouch of hers, because Mother Earth has allowed her to have that pouch. *It works–so it exists.*

What we observe every day represents, in a way, the sum of all *Past-Nows*. That's Mother Earth changing– *living, breathing.* That's *Evolution*," the Old Rabbit looked closely at his pupil. "The tricky bit is that we, as individual creatures–or 'Be-ings' (interesting word, that?)– all exist *within* one, infinitesimally-short instant of Time called *The Now* or, *The Moment;* and, therefore, we naturally think that everything we see is completed or *finished.*

But, it isn't, you see. All life is on an infinite journey of change, Tilly, " sweeping his gnarled paw across the meadow. "Just like that thistledown floating along over there", pointing. "Who knows where it came from, or where it will go from here– from N*ow*?

I am considered 'Old', as far as Rabbits, Hares, and maybe Polecats are concerned. But what of trees? My lifetime is but a blink to them. Quite strange, don't you think?"

The Old Rabbit noted the beginnings of a confused look creeping across Tilly's face and quickly said, "Perhaps I can better answer your question, though, by asking one of my own: Does a butterfly's two weeks on this Earth amount to anything less than a 'full life', as far as the butterfly is concerned? If a creature 'lives' within every instant– that is, within every *now moment* of its existence– does 'Time' actually exist for that creature?"

A brief silence passed as he allowed this latest thought to sink in.

"When we talk about Time, Tilly, aren't we really speaking of the *passage* of Time?

But what happens if Time *stands still?* Does it still exist? Is a river still a river, if it doesn't flow?"

A few long moments passed.

"If our fluttering friend over there," pointing to the brightly-colored butterfly gracefully floating upon a breezy current, "lives her entire life within unconnected instants, is Time actually 'passing' *in her mind?* Think about it, Tilly.

Our physical bodies suffer the ravages of 'aging'– storing *physical Past-Nows,* in effect," the old bunny wincing from his arthritis as if to make his point. "It shouldn't come as a surprise, then, that our brains also *store the past*– only with a few extra twists– the major difference being that it takes many months after we're born for our brain to develop its ability to 'store' memories– our *mental Past-Nows.*

"Do you remember anything from when you were a baby Rabbit, Tilly? If you don't, you're in good company. Not many of us do. That's because we are born into this world, prematurely. The outside layer of our brains, called the *Neo-Cortex* or 'New Layer', just like our bones, needs time to grow and mature. We are quite literally, 'born undercooked', Tilly! The Old Rabbit's eyes twinkled down tenderly upon the bunny like evening stars.

"Until your brain has a chance to figure out that it *exists*, Tilly, you're much the same as that butterfly over there– *existing solely in the Now–* and totally unaware of Time.

The catch is, that in order for your big, immature brain to understand that it actually exists, it must first learn *how to remember–* What happened to it yesterday? An hour ago? A second ago?

Think about it, Tilly: Our memories are what *glue* our Past and our Now together! Pretty fascinating, eh?"

CHAPTER 2

"**U**p for playing a thought game, Tilly?"

...and I thought that's what we were playing all along... Thought games within a thought game? My head hurts!

"What do you suppose would happen if, starting tomorrow morning, every Rabbit in the world instantly lost their ability to 'remember' anything that happened more than one minute ago? (that's about the length of a goldfish's memory, by the way). You'd wake up without any 'history', wouldn't you? No recollection of yesterday, let alone last week or last year! With no memories to refer to, wouldn't all Rabbits simply be living pretty much instant-by-instant, like our butterfly friend over there? Blissfully unaware of the past? We wouldn't know how old we are, or even that we had ever been born!

"So here's the tricky bit" *always seems to be one of those...*

"Even though our memories do connect our past with our present," Mr. Brambles continued, "I suspect that we Rabbits, nonetheless, actually *'exist'* only in the present moment. Just like every other living creature, our lives are effectively only a single instant long, Tilly... Are you feeling quite alright?"

Her head was beginning to feel a bit woolly, inside.. and wobbly, outside– Just barely balancing on her shoulders at the 'moment', as a matter of fact. She smiled at the irony.

Taking her smile as a "Yes", Mr. B continued, "So, the existence of Time appears to require some sort of memory reference point, doesn't it?

Ask yourself this, Tilly: Does a boat really *move* if the water it's in is moving at the same speed and in the same direction as the boat?

I'll grant you that if you happen to be standing on the shore watching, then the boat *is moving*. But if you are in the boat, it isn't really moving from the water's point of view, is it? Interesting, no?

Have you ever noticed how some days simply 'fly by'–the hours seeming like minutes? Other days that seem to 'drag on' *forever?"* winking, "especially when you're doing school work?"

Or like now, maybe...

"It's almost as though your brain *sees* things differently than what the clock is telling you, eh? *"Here's a little secret, Tilly."*

...my undercooked brain somehow feels quite overcooked at the 'moment'...

"What scientists' measure as *precise Time*– using their atomic clocks– has absolutely *nothing* to do with your brain's *perception* of Time. It's like having two different watches–one in your head, and one on your wrist."

OK. Her head was now in serious danger of exploding!

The Old Rabbit must have noticed saying, "I know how confusing this all must be for you, Tilly. My head sometimes feels like it's going to explode... Does that ever happen to you, by any chance?"

CHAPTER 3

He sensed the need for a diversion and deftly snatched up a nearby stone. "Just like the mother Kangaroo's pouch, Tilly, what you see here is not what this stone once looked like a million moon-turns ago, nor what it will look like in a million more."

With a bit of a hop-skip-and-jump, the Old Rabbit flourished, "I hereby proclaim that this rock I hold before you was once a comet!"

Tilly's eyes grew noticeably bigger.

"Just imagine it, Tilly! A dazzlingly brilliant, white streak blazing across the night sky fifty million moon-turns ago, fixing every creature's stare with its wondrous light!"

"I further proclaim that before becoming a comet, the atoms in this," holding up the sparkling stone for Tilly's closer examination, "belonged to a distant planet which broke up under the huge gravitational forces exerted upon it by its binary suns. Before the planet's demise, however, some of these atoms had once been part of a giant spiky worm living there, and in turn, an ancient insect-like bird who later dined on the unfortunate helminth... Sumptuous dinner, indeed!"

A long silence followed as the Old Rabbit watched Tilly assimilate his fantastical yarn... "and round-and-round it would have gone forever had it not been for the planet's destruction."

"If my Rock-Comet fancy is correct– and no one can prove it's not– then my comet, travelling across the galaxy, finally hit the ground as a meteorite, Hmmm... Right.. About.. Here!" the Old Rabbit bending down and replacing the rock with flamboyant care wherefrom he had first plucked it up.

"Atoms cycling forever, Tilly, means infinite possibilities. You see, it's all one big circular riddle, Life is. And that's why my head is in a constant state of near explosion!

Observe, Tilly! I hold a planet in my paw!"

Tilly smiled broadly at the Old Rabbit's theatrical flair.

CHAPTER 4

Mr. Brambles' thoughts, as they often did these days, now raced ahead of him, like a galloping, riderless horse out of control.

Speaking more to himself than to Tilly, he mumbled, *"Imagine all this from the Universe's perspective... 'Life' is merely an instantaneous manifestation within an infinitesimally small anomalous 'Eddy of Time', swirling round-and-round, within an infinitely long river of Time– Called 'Forever'.*

"For all intents and purposes, then, our instantaneous Eddy of Life within which we live, is rendered non-existent, relatively speaking, when placed next to the infinitely large and small scales of our Universe– If you don't have a reference point by which to compare something, you can't measure

it, now can you?

"And Infinity, by definition, has no reference point. We're just a glitch... All of life is just a simple glitch!"

Tilly couldn't quite follow all of Mr. Bramble's rapid-fire ramblings.

"Clearly, in such a situation," the Old Rabbit continued unabated, *"we can't directly apply the 'physical rules' of our existence– divined as they are on our scale– to the infinite scale of the Universe. Well, we can...and do. But we certainly shouldn't expect them to work! Yet that's precisely what we've been doing– A 'reverse-engineering/backwards-reasoning "Hat Trick– in the Sciences for centuries now, successfully wooing ourselves into believing a stupendously false self-serving 'Reality'... And ALL made possible courtesy of, Yes, you guessed it– Our big brain's unavoidable egocentric creation of Time!"* his hooting frightening the little wrens hopping around on the branches above.

"Ho Ho," the Old Rabbit openly chuckled. *"The rules of Time work for Rabbits, not for the Universe you doddering old fool! It's crystal clear–Has been all the time! Subtract Time from the equation, and the whole' Measurable Universe' sham falls down like a house of 'Find-a-Carrot' cards. Oh, how we've been fooling ourselves on a grand scale, Mr. Brambles. Ohh, how grand, indeed."*

CHAPTER 5

Tilly's head jerked up, having nodded off– hopefully for only a moment or two (*or was that yesterday's lecture she'd just been dreaming about?* Her head felt far too "over-inflated" for that to be the case, she decided).

"...So, once we Rabbits figured out– with the benefit of our brain's newly-evolved memory– that we actually *existed*," droned Mr. B, "we would have also realized that *we cease to exist*, as well.

Death! The Grim Grabber, Tilly." The Old Rabbit's face took on a now-familiar theatrical, haunted-house twist–"OOOH AHHRG, HA HA HA!", playfully affecting the actions of a particularly frightening ghoul.

Now fully animated, the Old Rabbit raced along again. "I believe that's when we *invented* such concepts as '*Time*' and '*God*', Tilly. If you think about it, a God's best trick is to side-step Time, isn't it?

"Voila! I give you, Immortality!" Another grand magician's flourish-of-paw accompanied this conclusion. "In fact, these 'Inventions' are an attempt to answer the next logical question our big brains must inevitably ask after becoming aware of death: *If I do exist, then Why do I exist?*

And that's the 64,000 carrot question, Tilly– *The one question* that every philosopher throughout history has sought to answer when putting pen to paper."

CHAPTER 6

"So, alas, we've come full circle, eh, Tilly?" The little bunny's sagging ears perked up perceptibly, hoping for the long-awaited conclusion.

"Isn't that what you first asked me? *"Why must we die?*

This will be my twelfth Summer, Tilly. Almost 150 moon turns– Think of that! Quite long for any Rabbit, and I've spent much of that time, Tilly, thinking about your question– and one other: *Where do I go when I die?*

Now, before I completely befuddle you..."

Befuddled doesn't begin to describe my brain right now.

"I'm going to tell you one last secret, rather more important than all the others we've ever spoken of before", the little bunny's ears ticking up another notch.

"After all my study of death– all my ear-twisting over the subject– I'm beginning to believe that when I die, my *Now Moment*– within which I have always lived as a Rabbit– *simply ends*. Full stop. I just jump into that 'Giant Top Hat in the Sky' and pop out again as part of something else, returning to the universal pool of infinitely-cycling atoms, with unlimited possibilities provided by "Infinite Time" (the World's biggest oxymoron, by the way).

"Actually." The Old Rabbit's face brightened, "I quite fancy myself becoming part of a Giant Spiky Fern Tree on some distant tropical planet– one with legs to walk around on, of course. And later, perhaps part of a dazzling comet." He looked down at the sparkling stone lying in his paw." *When had he picked that up again?* "Yeesss. I do very much fancy that possibility."

Although she fought it, Tilly's eyelids grew heavier and heavier as she fell headlong into the warm, dark embrace of sleep.

The Old Rabbit smiled sadly and slipped from the gnarled Elm root, whispering softly into Tilly's ear, "By the way young lady, I needn't remind you that you must never voice these, or any other of our 'crack-pot theories', to anyone– Never. Doing so will very likely land you in a home for bongo bunnies and unhinged hares, where you'll likely not be heard from again."

"OooKaay, Mr. Brambles," Tilly mumbled as she drifted away.

He glanced down, sadly, one last time at the tiny bunny, his precious pupil and friend, now snoring softly upon the tender grass, lulled by the pleasant drone of honeybees in her ears and the sweet smells of Spring tickling her nose.

Upon waking that morning, the Old Rabbit had somehow known that it had arrived– The Time to collect his few, important belongings from this life– and take the next step in his journey.

"Poor little tacker. I do feel a bit guilty– really I do– for pouring her head so full of weighty ideas, only a fraction of which she'll probably understand. No choice in the matter, however, no choice, did I have.

Oh, why can't I just get old like other Rabbits?" he grumbled. "Why can't I simply be satisfied with watching my Great Grandbunnies romp about while my old bones soak up the sunshine?"

The following morning, long before the sun poked its head above the rim of the world, he arose quietly. Slipping from his snug, warm burrow he carried a small, tightly-stuffed pouch strapped to his knotty walking stick, polished smooth by long years of service.

In the dim pre-dawn light, the Old Rabbit strode

carefully up the narrow, well-worn footpath that led beyond the Warren which had always been his home.

CHAPTER 7

A week passed and the little bunny still hadn't seen hide nor hair of her friend.

Each day she climbed to the clearing where the ancient elm tree had stood beyond collective memory, it's broad, outstretched arms harvesting the Sun's warmth. Each time she hoped beyond hope to find Mr. B there studying some new plant or bug he'd discovered, only to be disappointed, yet again.

She felt the tendrils of sadness growing deeper within her soul.

It's not the same happy place anymore without Mr. Brambles, she sniffled.

Now, you may not know this, Dear Reader, but Rabbits are quite different from other animals in several ways.

For example, at their core, most Rabbits are

fundamentally fun-loving creatures who avoid unhappiness by simply *choosing* not to participate in sad thoughts. Their memories, although long, can be remarkably selective, chronicling their past to suit themselves. In essence, they can't be bothered with remembering anything but "the fun parts" of life.

Therefore, when a Rabbit "disappears," for whatever reason–as had Mr. Brambles–well, no one really takes much notice. Sort of like disappearing and reappearing from a magician's hat. They'll be back at some point, so why worry?

As you may have guessed, however, Tilly wasn't your ordinary Rabbit. She was a very serious, inquisitive bunny, whose insatiable intellect, even at the age of two, was now far beyond that of most elder Rabbits in the Warren. It had always, both, confused and delighted her to think that Mr. B had taken a personal interest, confident enough in her abilities to share his many and varied "weird ideas".

These days, she almost *felt* his presence in her mind.

Although, Mr. B had always been referred to by others as the "Old Hare-Brained Professor," Tilly suspected quite the opposite. She had learned many things from the Old Rabbit, but foremost he had taught her *how* to think about things.

Strangely, she was discovering that his many eccentric lessons were starting to make more and more sense the older she got.

A sudden chilly breeze rattled the little bunny's spine, her sharp eyes simultaneously capturing a flicker just beyond one of the innumerable elm roots.

Curiosity piqued, Tilly hopped over to the base of the huge tree. Its earthy, moist smells washed over her senses, brushing against some deep, primordial appendage of her brain.

She carefully prodded the thick, wrinkled bark to discover a slight indentation where a tiny scrap of brilliantly orange paper flapped. In fact, it looked very much like the colored paper which Mr. Brambles always seemed to magically whip out of thin air at "opportune teaching moments," as he referred to them.

How could I have not noticed that before? she wondered.

In the same moment, as she had been diligently taught, an alternative thought flashed into her mind: *Had Mr. B returned and left some sort of message for her?*

Tilly tugged at the paper sliver until it ripped, leaving a smidgeon still lodged in the tree. *Almost as if it had been slipped through a slit in the bark... but so tightly? Strange.*

If she had learned anything from Mr. B's innumerable "Thought Games," it was to first always consider the least improbable, most simple possibility by which to explain an observation. The Old Rabbit had long insisted that the simplest explanations for something usually went unnoticed by most everyone; namely, because their minds didn't ever stop long enough to consider them.

When the giant honeybee nest in the Old Willow Snag by the creek had started shaking and the bees had angrily swarmed everywhere, all the Rabbits scampered into their burrows, quivering in fear, certain that the Earth would soon begin to shake under them, as well...That is, everyone except "Old Hare-Brained" Mr. B, who calmly walked around the back side of the twisted snag to discover the true "Earth shaker" to be, none other than, a very large and hungry black bear bent on finding his evening meal! *Simple explanation. Case solved!*

That had made quite an impression on young Tilly– It had, indeed.

And then there was the time when certain tasty morsels had turned up missing from the community storehouse the week prior to the annual harvest celebration. Poor Mr. Waddles, having the ill-fortune of being the Warren's "caretaker of stores" for that week, immediately became the key suspect in this heinous, "crime of the century".

You see, Rabbits can be quite vicious. Oh Yes. Fluffy, cute little creatures that they are... But where sweet juicy carrots, honey-filled bees' wax, and sugar beets are involved...Watch out!

Fits of extreme jealousy are well reported in Rabbit psychiatry journals, often manifesting themselves when a Rabbit believes that someone else is getting something yummy that they're not. Well... Poor little Waddles!

Mr. Brambles, thankfully, was equally convinced of Mr. Waddles' innocence, if only because, in his estimation, this simple little Rabbit was wholly incapable of contemplating such a daring deed (you see, Waddles frequently suffered embarrassing episodes of fainting associated with encountering his own shadow in the late afternoon sunshine).

No, Waddles was far too timid to risk such a theft, in Mr. B's considered opinion.

In any event, just before the angry mob was set to pluck every whisker from poor Mr. Waddles' quivering cheeks for his dastardly crime (no worse punishment can be conceived of for a Rabbit, by the way), Mr. Brambles stepped forward with, what for Mr. Waddles, was literally a "face-saving" explanation:

ANTS! Yes. That's right– Bugs!

Of course no one had thought of such a simple possibility, and none were too quick to entertain the idea at that point, having the scent of blood in their noses and singularly bent on a "public plucking".

So the Old Rabbit proposed a novel experiment for the following night to prove "beyond the shadow of an Owl's whisker, that the true culprit in this despicable theft was, in fact, a band of renegade formicidae.

Sure enough, and to Mr. Waddles' considerable relief, next morning's light demonstrated a conspicuous absence of the tasty morsels which had been strategically left overnight as bait in the locked store house.

There were those amongst the vigilante Disciplinary Committee who appeared more than a wee bit disappointed by what they saw when Mr. Brambles unlocked the storeroom door that morning– for it had been a good long while, after all, since they'd enjoyed a good whisker-pulling.

This actually worked out quite well, by the way, for not only a hugely-relieved Mr. Waddles, but for Mr. Brambles' tummy, wherein the tasty tid-bits then resided!

Oh, it's not what you think. It's just that the Old Rabbit knew his various species of ants well enough to understand that the particular variety of ants guilty of the crime were diurnal, not nocturnal, and probably wouldn't have shown up in time to save poor Waddles' whiskers. Besides being innately jealous, Rabbits tend to be rather impatient creatures, as well, and Mr. Brambles knew that his fellow denizens would not have waited a second beyond the crack of dawn to prove or disprove his six-legged theory. So the only logical solution left to him was to eat the morsels and end the matter!

All's well that ends well, I suppose. Tilly chuckled at the thought of the Old Rabbit hopping around the moonlit storeroom gobbling up the yummy delicacies!

What a very strange Old Rabbit, Mr. Brambles was– *IS!* Tilly caught herself– with his ancient magnifier always at the ready, conjured at a moment's notice from some secret pocket in his well-worn waistcoat, to examine something interesting he'd just discovered.

She recalled fondly his many pockets, invariably brimming over with pencils, rulers, bits of old chewing gum and string ("always be prepared, that's my motto, Tilly") – his burrow walls lined with dusty, well-thumbed books.

Now that she thought of it, no one in the Warren, other than Mr. Brambles, even owned a book!

Tilly blinked back a tear, swallowing hard.

CHAPTER 8

A small gust of wind turned her mind back toward the bit of paper fluttering in her paw.

What would Mr. Brambles have concluded about this paper if he were standing here?

Of course, the most obvious conclusion would have to be that the ancient elm tree was hollow, but that would be silly, she laughed. Wouldn't it?

I swear I just heard the Old Rabbit quietly chuckling in my head...

And in that instant, she knew it must be true.

Why else would he have left this piece of paper behind (and she had no doubt that he had) if not to serve as a clue– a test for her?

For the first time, the young Rabbit began to examine the massive tree in earnest.

It struck her as odd that after all the days spent

playing in the clearing around the Old Elm she had never really fully appreciated its enormity.

The towering branches she now peered up through seemed to span the entire meadow. So dense was its canopy that the sky was, in places, completely obscured by its verdant foliage.

She began to systematically exam every nook and cranny of the massive tree's trunk. She pushed and prodded every knot and divot that her little paws came across.

She was carefully picking her way through the twisted roots when she noticed something shiny halfway into one of the many darkened niches. On closer inspection, this turned out to be another shiny section of tree root.

Just how, pray tell, does a section of root so far back in a dingy recess like this one, get polished smooth?

"Good question, Til," she mumbled to herself.

I'd better stop answering myself or they'll lock me away for sure.

As she began to shimmy back out of the tight recess she smiled to herself. *That rascally Old Rabbit is certainly having his fun with me today, he is...*

After a more thorough investigation, Tilly decided that the only logical answer was that the root must be another seat, like the one the Old Rabbit always sat on with her during their lessons.

She was deep in thought, contemplating possibilities, when a loud rumbling interrupted her– which turned out to be her tummy! She realized it was well past her supper, three hours having slipped by like three minutes...Just like Mr B had said!

She decided to hurry home and return after dark to continue her sleuthing. Retracing her steps through the maze of twisted roots, Tilly made careful mental notes to assist upon her return.

CHAPTER 9

The full moon rose above the hill top in all its splendor as Tilly filled her tummy with the fresh beet-root, crispy carrot tops and yummy parsnips that her mother had expertly prepared.

Delectable! Nothing makes a Rabbit happier than dining on a farmer's fresh vegetables under the light of a full moon. It's what bunny dreams are made of– Truly magical stuff.

Tilly could barely contain her excitement during supper– but knew she must. Otherwise, her parents would suspect something was afoot and start asking unwanted questions.

She politely excused herself from the table early, citing a pending school assignment that required attention (Oh, yes, bunnies must attend a minimum of two and one quarter years of formal education).

Back in her room, she packed a few items in her old burlap tramping bag, including her beloved soft lamb's wool jumper that her mother had knitted for those cold winter nights. The wool had been collected for over a year from farmer's fences where the sheep regularly rub.

At the last moment, she pocketed the old, burnished pen knife Mr. B had given her, along with a paw-full of dried Sweet Drop berries that would hopefully keep her stomach preoccupied. (Yes. Rabbits must eat every 2-3 hours if they're to remain bright-eyed and bushy-tailed!). She was ready for her sleuthing adventure!

Silently feeling her way along the smooth earthen walls of their ancient burrow, Tilly was soon out into the crisp night air. She smiled knowing that Mr. Brambles would have definitely approved!

Quietly hopping up the hardened footpath, she soon reached the top of the knoll, with the partial outline of the Old Elm clearly visible across the meadow below.

The moon shimmered its glorious light across the meadow, silvering the ground like a skiff of newly-fallen snow. Suddenly a darkened figure slid through the shadowy sky. Tilly stood frozen, raw fear clutching her brain.

CHAPTER 10

The patient owl had spied his prey as it bounded up the trail. He remained stock-still in his tree-top post until the small Rabbit had hopped from beneath the tree cover well into the open. Now the young tender morsel stood frozen, *just as all little furry creatures will do in such situations,* he smiled knowingly, making it an easy kill. The Owl did this sort of thing all the time and was, in truth, rather bored with the routine. His stomach, however, demanded regular attention, so repeat the procedure, he must.

As always, he congratulated himself on fighting back the urge to swoop prematurely and possibly miss out on dinner for being over-hasty.

He felt the familiar pleasure growing in his tummy. He snapped his beak automatically once or twice in anticipation of the evening meal that awaited him below.

The bunny could not escape. There was no cover within a hundred bounds (a Rabbit's bound being approximately two-and-one-half human feet). The original panic that had frozen Tilly's brain now began to thaw. Her mind began to slowly turn over the situation and consider any options that might present themselves. Still, she remained stock-still.

She knew she could not run, as that would only facilitate the Owl's immediate swoop and certain death.

"That would put you at a distinct disadvantage," came the Old Rabbit's unsolicited voice. *"...Your not being able to see your pursuer coming from behind, that is."*

"Then what should I do?" she whispered.

"If you can't find cover, then wait." came the advice. The ridiculousness of the suggestion caught her off guard.

Wait! For what, pray tell me? A divine, well-aimed thunderbolt perhaps? noting the crisp clear night sky. She remained statuesque, however, while her presence-of-mind steadily flowed back to her.

By this time the Owl was rather enjoying the young Rabbit's obvious paralysis, feeling quite pleased with himself. He relished his apparent complete dominance over the tiny quivering creature below.

"Fear gotten the best of your senses, eh, my little

tasty bunny? A shame, that. I'd have rather enjoyed a bit of a challenge before eating this night," said the Owl, who now abandoned any attempts at stealth. He continued his flight on a leisurely, round-about course towards his incapacitated prey. Truth be told, this rather annoyed the owl since he had waited for nearly three nights in the top of the spruce tree for this chance at one of the plump little creatures frolicking about below.

Field mice had quickly become bland, interim snacks, and now he realized his reward for all his patience would only be a tiny rendition of his fat visions– and a fear-struck one, at that!

Where's the fun in that? he said to himself, as he slowly winged towards the young Rabbit. Once this one turns up missing and its remains are discovered, an all-out owl alarm would race throughout the countryside, severely limiting any further hunting opportunities in the foreseeable future.

This, along with an admixture of tangential hunger-driven thoughts, meandered through the Owl's mind as he continued his lazy course towards the marble bunny.

"If you can't find any cover, improvise! Use your own!" came the voice.

It took Tilly a very long second to understand this latest advice, by which time the whites of the Owl's wing feathers had become clearly recognizable. Everything seemed to be proceeding in *slow-motion* to the little bunny. *Hah!* She recalled the Old Rabbit's lecture, the pointy irony not escaping Tilly's fully-thawed brain.

At the very last moment, just as she saw the huge glistening yellow talons opening above her, Tilly grasped the heavy woolen jumper to her chest, and dove for the small swale in the ground her brain had somehow registered lying just a few feet in front of her. In that instant, she rolled onto her back and extended the woolen jumper upward to meet the huge claws which immediately sunk into the thick layers of wool. One talon penetrated through the jumper and partially sunk into the fur and flesh of the little bunny's right shoulder.

Tilly screamed, more in fear than pain, sending a deeply primitive reverberation of pleasure through the Owl's brain.

The giant bird now flapped skyward, all other thoughts abandoned. He grasped the woolen jumper tightly in anticipation of a lovely snack!

It briefly flitted across the Owl's mind on the journey back to the spruce tree that his prey should be struggling a bit more but, then again, it had been so frightened in the meadow that it couldn't move, so why fight now? *Poor creature may well have simply died of fright,* he postulated, continuing on his flight towards his needled perch.

CHAPTER 11

The instant Tilly dove and covered herself, the owl's talons had ripped the burlap bag, and the jumper it contained, into the night sky. The sting in her right shoulder now brought her mind into perfect synchrony with the moment, allowing her to focus on the pain.

"Run! Now! While you have the time and strength. RUN!"

She jumped up and scampered through the meadow faster than she had ever hopped before. Seconds before she reached the safety of the Old Elm, she heard the angry screech of the Owl slice the crisp night air.

The screams quickly escalated beyond the edges of primitive fury, upon his discovering that nothing edible lived within the burlap bag. The Owl clawed back into the night sky, viciously pounding the air with his wings in a wild search for his escaped victim.

Instead of the two or three final bounds it should have taken her to cover the remaining distance to the Elm, Tilly crossed the space in a single, super-bunny leap timed perfectly with the Owl's frustrated screams.

She dove head-first into a crevice formed by the roots and squirreled her way through the maze at speeds that astonished even her. She somehow ended up panting, sitting on the very same shiny root she had discovered only that afternoon– *What are the odds...?*

"How very comfortable this little seat is, indeed!" she said out loud, surprised by the calm that had descended over her.

Although, quite exhausted and with a painful shoulder that throbbed terribly Tilly, nonetheless, concentrated on controlling her breathing while she listened intently for any signs of further danger.

Satisfied that the duped Owl had not followed her into the root-maze, Tilly relaxed. She popped two more Sweet Drop berries into her mouth while she considered her current predicament. With exhaustion now rapidly catching up, her eyelids began to sag and the old shiny root was becoming the most comfortable chair she'd ever sat in.

Tilly was distantly aware that something important had changed. She was a different Rabbit now– somehow transformed by the evening's frightful ordeal. She vaguely sensed this internal shift, but didn't know exactly what had changed in her, or what it meant.

"You are now, and forever more, in control of your own destiny, my little friend," chuckled the now familiar disembodied voice.

Her eyes blinked one final time and closed, the throb in her shoulder lessening as the young Rabbit drifted off into a deep, dreamless sleep.

CHAPTER 12

Down, down she fell, as the Old Owl's talons released her from far above the Earth's rocky countenance, its razor-sharp craggy teeth ready to receive her. Wait! Wasn't that a stack of soft woolen jumpers just there? Over there. Yes! My only hope!

Tilly struggled and squirmed to redirect her fall but wasn't moving fast enough in the right direction! She was going to hit the rocks! Only seconds now...

She gasped awake, clutching at the empty air above her before abruptly hitting the ground below the shiny root that had only moments before served as her bed.

It took her brain a few moments to organize the jumbled thoughts now starting to cascade down like a waterfall.

Through the Elm's low-hanging branches, Tilly noted the large, pendulous moon now loitering on the opposite horizon. Its yellow light eerily dappled the tangled elm roots, confirming the early morning hour. "The Sun's almost up," she murmured, the night's events seeming only a distant, shadowy recollection.

Again, she sniffed the air and listened intently for any signs of danger. Satisfied, she casually looked around the base of the tree, popping another delicious Sweet Drop berry in her mouth to stave off her 'rumbly' tummy's complaints.

These berries always seem to help me think, don't they? Perhaps there was a botanical book in Mr. B's library that would explain that? She tucked the thought away for later research.

The wavering moonlight cast pleasing shadows across the tree's massive trunk, revealing nuances that Tilly had not noticed the previous day. For the first time, the young Rabbit took serious note of the seemingly endless creases and depressions that made up the Old Elm's wizened bark. Crawling closer, she wished she had the benefit of Mr. Brambles' old looking glass with which to study the smaller details.

With each inch she drew closer, her eyes grew wider, as what she saw became progressively clearer.

It couldn't be! NO WAY!

CHAPTER 13

B ut it was.

Tilly realized something was written– more like, *grown*– within the pattern of the bark that could only be recognized at this exact distance from the tree, and at this specific time under a full moon's light!

In a queer text, Tilly read: "You have arrived at The Portal– Wait– It will show you The Way"

Who had left this message? The Tree? "Oh, Get Real! Who is this *It*, anyway? And what might 'It' be trying to show me?" she said out loud.

Her head swam with possibilities. For a fleeting moment, she even considered that this could all be the work of Malbunz– the unruly Warren bully who always seemed to be at the bottom of most of the Warren's unexplained "incidents". *Silly thought.*

CHAPTER 14

Tilly briefly toyed with the idea of attempting a scamper back to her cozy burrow, but the possibility of the Owl waiting out in the meadow somehow changed her mind.

"Not yet daybreak. Better hold off on that plan for the moment," she whispered to herself.

She leaned back on the shiny root and awaited the Sun's warm debut, which she guessed would be in about thirty minutes. (Not surprisingly, Rabbits have developed quite sophisticated senses of natural cycles, depending heavily on the Moon to define growing seasons, etc.)

The weary moon had continued its slow descent, resting now upon the Earth's edge like a colossal pale night orchid, its long night's pilgrimage nearly at an end. Tilly watched with passing interest as the light slowly focused through a series of specific triangles formed by the various tree roots. As she watched, the moonlight's silhouette sullenly crept along the trunk of the great tree until, only seconds before sinking below the horizon, it fell upon a small darkened corner beneath a dense tangle of roots. The words were immediately, if only momentarily, visible: *"Loqueris ad Portam Magnam"*.

CHAPTER 15

While the warm orb of the sun brimmed over the eastern horizon, countering the loss of the erstwhile moon, Tilly quickly backed out of the tight root recess and scampered across the now sunlit meadow– keeping a sharp eye trained on the spruce tree... *Yes, that would bear watching in the future.*

When she arrived home, her mother looked up from the breakfast table and said, "There you are Tilly. Did you see Mr. Simpy, per chance, on your hop? Wasn't it cold out there? Where in heaven's name is your woolen wrap I made for you? Honestly Tilly, you really should try to start thinking ahead".

Oh... if you only knew... instead saying, "No, Mother, he wasn't outside, at least not where I was," attempting to dodge any further questions by heading to her bedroom.

"Hold on there, young lady." Tilly's heart nearly stopped mid-beat, as her father gave her a stern look. She was caught! She knew they'd figure it out sooner or later, and now she'd had it...

"You must eat your breakfast before you run off anywhere else, Little Bunny."

SHAZZAM! YUMMY!! She happily gobbled down the fresh sweet tubers, crispy carrot tops (it's a common misconception that Rabbits prefer carrots to carrot tops) and raisins– courtesy of Old Farmer Bilstien's grape arbor– her mother had placed in front of her.

Back in her room, she rifled through her "everything box"– the receptacle for all varieties of gizmos, mechanisms, and unique trinkets– which she kept hidden beneath her bed.

She pocketed a tiny magnifying glass, a small lead pencil, several blank sheets of school paper, and a box of stick matches, rushing back to the kitchen to fill the remainder of her school knapsack (her old burlap bag, no doubt, currently residing somewhere at the top of a conifer tree) with various tasty items from the pantry.

She was just planning to bolt out the front door when she heard, *"And just where do you think you're going, Missy...?"* Tilly froze.

"You have a fair few chores which require your attention this morning, young lady, including tidying up that root cellar, and sweeping the front path. When you've finished with those, I've a few inside jobs I'd like your help with, as well."

OHH Drats! Rats! and Smelly Old Bats! Her mother always seemed to have at least two more things to do no matter how much she did!

Tilly's previously perky ears sagged visibly to the floor as she turned back towards her room, where she deposited the overstuffed knapsack on her bed and headed downstairs to the root cellar. *UGGUH!! Not having fun!!*

She hadn't even begun to sweep the cellar floor of the many dried root bits when she heard her father come down the tunnel towards her.

Oh, Great. That's all I need right now– More things that Father "would appreciate my help" doing.

"Hello Lassy! And how are you this fine day? I thought you and I might go collect some water-chestnuts up at Baggsly Lake later on this afternoon? When you've finish here, of course. It would be heaps of fun, and tasty too!"

That's it! I'm NEVER going to get back up to the Old Elm Tree at this rate!

Dejection set in.

Tilly considered feigning a tummy ache and, perhaps then, *they'd leave me alone long enough to make my escape?*

Great idea except for Old Doctor Brairy, whom

her parent would certainly send for... and He *always* made you swallow some foul-tasting concoction, irrespective of your symptoms. Not to mention his highly unpleasant, smelly, gooey poultices and potions, concocted from heaven only knew what!

Actually, Tilly smiled to herself, *that's probably why more bunnies didn't complain of feeling sick– too frightened by the prospect of a visit from the old quack!*

We'll skip that plan for now, she decided.

"Why did all medicines have to taste so terrible, anyway?" she pondered plaintively.

Should have asked Mr. B that question, making yet another mental note to study the problem in the future. *IF THERE IS A FUTURE, that is, beyond all these chores!*

There was always the outside chance that Grandpoppy would drop by, as he did some weekends, for a chin-wag with Father, at which point she could sneak out unnoticed.

Low Associated Probability (LAP), Tilly assessed. *There must be a way out of this situation!*

Mr. Brambles had always been quite firm on this particular point, pronouncing that "There are always at least two solutions to every problem, Tilly. It is just a matter of locating one of them when you need it."

So she just had to *think* her way out of her current prison...

That's it! A bad headache from thinking too much (pretty close to the truth, actually). No one could blame her for that and she could take a nap to feel better. Bonus– No quack and no special medicines required!

Always a solution to any problem... Yes indeed!

CHAPTER 16

The first act of the melodrama began with Tilly catching her father's attention, slowly rubbing her temples. She squinted her eyes *just enough*, in *just the right way*, to make it appear as though she were trying *not* to show that her head *really* throbbed.

STRIKE! Her father took the bait– hook, line and sinker!

I've a career on the stage if ever I decide to give up Science...

"What's the problem, Tilly? Are your eyes bothering you? Headache, is that it?"

"You'd better let me sweep this while you go lie down in your room for a while. Oh, and on your way up, stop at the cooler and pour yourself a nice cold cup of carrot juice. That'll help soothe the pounding between your ears."

SCHIZZAMMO! The bonuses just kept rolling in! 'Critically Acclaimed Performance', indeed! Not just evading the chores, but a free glass of scrumptious carrot juice in the bargain!

In true thespian spirit, Tilly maintained the act to the bitter end, feebly protesting her father's directives. She half slurred her thanks, muttering something about dizziness, and that perhaps a long nap *might, indeed, help...* as she weakly leaned the broom against the cellar wall and drug her feet along the floor towards the upstairs burrow. She had to stop at least twice to dramatically catch her breath, and balance, before continuing her pitiful sojourn up the tunnel.

Around the bend in the upper passageway– and safely out of sight of her father– Tilly bounded gleefully to the pantry where she poured herself a mugful (the big brown glazed one her father always used for his tea) of cool, sweet carrot juice, then headed quickly to her room.

Planning ahead, she rolled up two pillows, sticking them conspicuously under her fluffy bed covers to make it appear to a casual glance that she was, indeed, slumbering deeply.

Really convincing would be a pillow that moved, rhythmically, up and down– like breathing in and out... Have to give that some serious creative attention at some point.

She grabbed her pack and scampered down the

hallway and out the front door before her father finished her chores in the cellar below. *Not getting waylaid again!*

The dulcet aroma of Mrs. Beezworth's parsnip strudel wafted by her nose from next door.

Oh, Sweet Moonbeams! How I'd love a bowl of that right now, her mouth watering as she bounded up the viney footpath.

CHAPTER 17

It was near midday when Tilly arrived back at the elm tree, with the Sun's warm rays ricocheting off peculiar angles dancing odd shadows amongst the great tree's roots. Tilly's fur felt comfortably warm.

It took her a few minutes to discover exactly which recess held the shiny root she'd discovered the day before. When she did finally locate the spot, it looked much the same in its perpetually shadowy state. Tilly proceeded to spread her "tools" on the ground and probe the bark seam which still held the bit of yellow paper.

"Snippity Do-Dah–Skippity Eh," she sang to herself as she worked. She giggled when she noticed the tiny honeybee buzz quizzically around her nose, no doubt thinking her little song belonged to another Bee creature.

"I like your song, as well, Sir Beezy Boo" she bowed with a flair to the little creature. *Yes! The stage awaits!*

The small, thin blade of the old pen knife slipped tightly into a hidden crevice within the Elm's bark, and Tilly carefully traced its course, moving the knife vertically until the blade stopped. She removed the blade and re-positioned its blade horizontally where she discovered a similar seam to trace along. This one demarcated a strange arched geometry representing what appeared to be the top of an apparent doorway.

Tilly stopped to see if she could make out any of the cryptic words she had previously noticed in the moonlight, but they were nowhere to be seen. *How interesting.*

"Okay. So now what are you going to do?"

...She hadn't asked the question. She was sure of it. Hadn't even thought it. Yet, she'd definitely *heard* it, and she didn't think it came from inside her head. *Or had it?*

Anything seemed possible these days.

"I don't know, actually. What would you suggest?" She answered flippantly, just on the off-chance she might be suffering from mad-hare disease.

"I don't know. You tell me, Bunny Girl!"

Tilly jumped at least a meter in the air, cracking her head on the overlying root in the process.

OUCH!!

Unnerved, her tiny voice quavered, "Who-who, ARE you?" She expected to awaken any moment back in her bed. *Maybe hitting my head on that root addled my brain...*

"Who do you think I am? Use that big bag of brains between your floppies, Bunny Girl."

Dead silence, as Tilly's brain simply froze solid.

"AHH, Sneezes! Wheezes! and Blue Bunny Cheeses!! That rascally Brambles promised me a smart one this time!" angrily retorted the disembodied voice.

Tilly was now nearly apoplectic. Completely paralyzed, she couldn't even manage a blink.

A small, green speckled tree ant crawled across her nose, taking the opportunity waggle its fuzzy head gear at her, obviously miffed by the rude dislodgement from its comfortable residence located on the overhanging root– The root Tilly had just conked her head on.

"Just wait until I see that old scruffy hopper again! I'll transmute him into a fat wombat, or maybe a key chain."

"On second thought, that's far too good for the likes of him– Too Simple. No, I believe something more... complex and dastardly... is in order for my fuzzy little friend. Hmmm... I'll have to think on that for a while. Could be fun now that I consider the possibilities!"

Just about then Tilly's nose began quivering uncontrollably, a sure sign that her brain was not far behind.

CHAPTER 18

The day grew tired. Even the collective bug-buzz– usually quite boisterous at that hour– was noticeably less energetic.

The fragrant, heavy-headed clover blossoms nodded low under the afternoon hot sun as Tilly sat beneath the Elm Tree in thought.

Unseen mythical creatures! Weren't those only conjured up by "creative" young bunnies to explain missing pantry treats? Or messes of unknown origin?

But such "invisible friends" were never taken seriously, were they? Not even by their creators.

Until now, that is.

Tilly was pretty certain she'd never convince anyone that this had really happened. After all, maybe it hadn't– just ghosts echoing from a conk-on-the-head, sort of thing.

If she were to tell someone about all this, well, she'd likely wake up wearing baggy floral clothing in some remote "Funny-Bunny Farm," being poked and prodded by stodgy old pince-nez-wearing Rabbits with bow ties, smelling of moth-balls. She could see them now, tutt-tutting about with clipboards, scribbling esoteric notes about the unique directional changes taken by her whiskers when subjected to various levels of electric shock.

Another chill rattled up the little bunny's spine. Tilly, smiling considered the uber-absurdity of her situation.

Might as well turn myself in now. Just lock me up and throw away the key. Get it over with.

The almost humorous notion struck her that, perhaps, she might, indeed, *be a couple of carrots short of a bunch*? After all, she had been talking to unseen voices, as of late?

She recalled the whispers she'd heard all her life about one strange distant relative or another.

Probably some combination of recessive "rogue mental genes" having fun with her brain, she mused.

A distant cousin came to mind, whose sincere faith in his ability to fly had led him to test his unfortunate theory, selflessly contributing yet another disproved theorem to the great annals of "The Annual Darwin Awards".

Oh, yeh. Funny– Almost.

There was that one story... told openly amongst her family, about her mother's Great Uncle Bombsy who, it is said, burned down his burrow (along with half the Warren) back in the drought years while experimenting in his cellar... something to do with a steam-powered rain-making machine, as she recalled?

Now that Tilly seriously confronted the "sanity" subject, hadn't there been a story bandied about "over-the-back-hedges" a few years back, involving some hare-brained old hermit relative who everyone swore was some sort of wizard*, and who had turned some unfortunate Rabbit into a Pickle-Nosed Toad for making an off-handed insult about his whiskers?

*You see, Rabbits have always thought of themselves, deep down, as the only true magical creatures on Earth (Fairies, excepted), being closely aligned with magicians, black top hats, and the like. This phenomenon, dubbed "Whimsical Mental Conjurations" (WMC), has been studied extensively in Leporid Psychiatry circles. According to WMC theory, if confronted with a bona fide magical situation, the overriding tendency for a Rabbit is to undergo an immediate "brain freeze"– the sine qua non for transcendence into the magical realm; hence, the reason why we Rabbits always seem so *still* in magical situations.

This, along with the bonus of possessing long, easily-grabbable ears, explains why Rabbits remain the preferred furry creature for snatching out of a top hats!

CHAPTER 19

We've already established that Tilly was no ordinary Rabbit. Not by any measure.

She knew her brain was "weird". Perhaps it had something to do with the fact that she had no brothers or sisters (unheard of in Rabbit litters, which usually number anywhere from eight to twelve "Kits"). Had she somehow inherited an extra large scoop of "weird genes"? Perhaps an entire litter's worth?

My parents always told me that I should be proud of the fact that I am, after all, the "only, only-bunny" ever born in Warren history. Funny, that...

She was, likewise, "quite special" in that she could remember things that she shouldn't have been able to remember.

But she did.

For instance, she recalled her mother laughingly exclaim "You are very active bunnies, you all are; certainly love to thump about".

The only problem was that her Mother had said it before Tilly was born.

She even remembered that her grandpoppy had been present at the time saying, "Yep. That's what they all said happened to your great grandmoppy before your great grandfather Bombsy's litter was hatched."

When Tilly had innocently asked about this conversation one night at the dinner table, her Mother had turned quite pale (quite a trick, you'll agree, for a pink-eyed, white Rabbit), and quickly changed the topic of discussion to, "Oh how beautiful the petunias and sunflowers have grown with all the rain this year..."

Tilly wasn't sure whether it was this, or the fact that she was born able to speak perfectly, that labeled her "special".

It goes without saying that the entire Rabbit colony seemed to treat her a bit differently than other bunnies, with the elders even giving her a noticeably wide berth when passing on footpaths. All except old eccentric Mr. Brambles, that is, who would regularly stop by Tilly's school room to take her for long-winded walks. They'd converse about everything from apiary management and the various honey flavors (Rabbits being keen bee-keepers, you see), to the arcane subjects of chemical reactions and the goings on inside stars and atoms.

Tilly had once overheard Old Mrs. Silliroot whispering to another Elder that, prior to Tilly, Mr. Brambles had never even spoken to a bunny.

No. Being "special" had its plusses and minuses, she decided.

CHAPTER 20

Tilly awoke to persistent urgings.

Someone, at quite regular intervals, was tugging on her floppy ears as they hung down over the sides of the shiny root where she had apparently fallen asleep.

"All right. You can stop that now, if you wouldn't mind," she mumbled irritably.

The pestiferous tugging continued, however, first one ear and then the other.

"Okay. That will be quite enough, whoever you are. I am thoroughly awake now."

Tilly looked with unveiled annoyance toward the ground as she sat up on the root.

She saw nothing, however, amongst the countless twisted roots below. She continued to stare intently into the surrounding gloom, her concerns growing with each second's passing.

"Oh dear, I do hope this isn't my busybody invisible friend at work again" speaking her concerns to the shadows.

"Nnnn-nope. Not me. I'm no dizzy-body, whatever that i-i-s, or even a ba-ba-busy one, for that ma-matter. I'm o-only a ma-messenger, supposed to ga-give you this pa-paper."

A slight whooshing sound preceded the tiny paper airplane's flight from one of the many shadowy caverns formed where the elm's roots met the ground.

A brief pause was followed by an immediate, muffled, *Ka-THUMP*, as if a small door had been slammed shut.

The little plane swirled upwards, expertly orbiting Tilly's head, brushing past her long whiskers before she snatched it from the air.

She took a deep breath, thinking, *Time I get off this crazy merry-go-round and think things through just a bit. Wouldn't take an egg-headed Einstein to figure out that someone was trying to tell you something, Tilly Girl.*

Unfolding the tiny aircraft, also apparently constructed from Mr. B's stiff orange paper, the analytic part of Tilly's brain admired the simplicity of the plane's butterfly-shaped wing design.

Written in clear, bold letters on the paper was: *Come on! Hurry up and open the door in the tree!*

She wasn't sure whether to laugh or..well..laugh?

What other alternatives were there?

It's verging on surreal silliness, now.

She knew where she had traced out the shape of a door in the bark, but how was she supposed to actually *open* it? The note failed to mention that little detail.

"He told me you were supposed to be a smart one," drifted back to her mind.

Another test of my intelligence, no doubt, I guess if I fail, I can always just go home and forget this ever happened, now can't I?

But she knew herself better than that. She'd never met a riddle she didn't like.

"Let's face it, I'm a victim of my own curiosity," she admitted with a smirk.

OK. I surrender. Come take me away. I'll go peacefully.

"There must be some sort of catch mechanism here somewhere", she observed. "And it would have to be located along the outline of the door, wouldn't it?"

She re-traced the door's outline once again with her knife, but no latches were apparent. Perhaps, the release mechanism is remotely located, like a certain root to be pulled, or a spring-loaded knot to be pushed?

She pushed and tugged on everything in the vicinity without result.

How else can a door be opened, anyway? Think!

She recalled an old bedtime story about a cave used by villains which opened only when you knew just the right words to say– in just the right order.

But that was only an imaginary bunny book, wasn't it? Just like invisible friends.

Could it be? The words she had seen in the briefly illuminated cavern the night before? Could they be the words needed to open the door?

Tilly stood on her hind legs, the shiny root proving a bit slippery. She looked in all directions for the mysterious words the dying moonlight had displayed within the darkened enclave. Nothing!

The lighting wasn't right and she couldn't wait another twelve hours to try and recreate the same circumstances. What *were* those four words? she wracked her brain.

Where is that lauded Big-Brained, "Past-Now-Storage expert" when I need you?

BANG! The words appeared crystal clear in her mind:

"Loqueris ad Portam Magnam"

She read the strange words verbatim from her brain's blackboard and was immediately rewarded by a sharp *CLICK*. She watched in utter amazement as the squeak of rubbing tree bark preceded a slowly gaping door, revealing the darkened interior of the Elm's massive trunk.

CHAPTER 21

At that very same moment, Tilly saw the snake out of the corner of her eye, its evil slithering form emerging from a nearby lair hidden beneath the twisted roots.

Tilly reflexively jumped directly into the tree's yawning interior, landing tail first. *Thank goodness for its fluffiness!*

There followed the now familiar swishing noise, followed by a quiet *CLUMP*, and inky darkness enveloped the little bunny.

I guess a secret door wouldn't stay secret very long if it didn't automatically close, Tilly thought, strangely unruffled by this latest event.

She briefly wondered whether repeating the cryptic words would open the door from inside the tree? *I suppose I really should take care not to forget the words... That is, if I ever plan on getting out of this tree.* She tried hard to swallow down the panic that was crawling up the back of her throat. "Probably wouldn't know where to find the door, anyway, after that tumble", she reasoned.

I'll just have to keep going, I suppose, feeling at least slightly reassured that this had to be someone's plan, after all.

Tilly felt along the tree's insides and found part of the surface unexpectedly smooth. She moved her paw up and down the wall to discover a well-defined band of smoothness measuring about a paw's width.

Excitement quickly replaced apprehension.

A pathway all marked out by others– about the same size as me!

Reassuring.

Guided by the wall's "paw-path", she set off without another thought, excitement and apprehension comingling into a congealed sense of purpose. She was about to find out what awaited her at the other end of this tree-tunnel– *And that was SUPER EXCITING!*

CHAPTER 22

After what seemed like an hour (or a week?) of shuffling along in utter lightlessness, Tilly was forced to conclude that she couldn't possibly still be inside the great Elm Tree. *How could that be? I didn't go up or down.* "Could I be going in circles?" she said out loud.

"Don't be daft, Bunny Girl"

Once again, Tilly's spinal reflex arcs sparked and she jumped straight up in the air. *At least no root to smack my head on this time– That's something, anyway.*

"Oh, it's you again, is it? What do you want now? All you ever do is say mean things about my intelligence or my fur. So why don't I just ignore you?"

"Ahhh. So you do have a bit of spunk under all that fuzz, after all."

"There. You see? You've done it again! You are annoying!"

Why not tell me something of value– like, where to find a light switch around here or, even better, where's the pantry? I'm starving!"

"Figure it out yourself, Fur Bag."

Disgusted, Tilly promised herself to simply ignore any more of, whatever It-Is's derogatory comments.

The murkiness grew darker, not lighter– if that was possible– the further Tilly shuffled along the tunnel. It was more of a feeling than an actual perception, she decided.

She felt very alone.

With the exception of a few "Creaks" and "Groans", no other sounds interrupted her journey.

Total isolation eating at her resolve, Tilly still soldiered on, driven by her unspoken faith in the Mr. B. She *had* to believe it was his plan. Where was she going to go otherwise? Back?

Besides, where *was* back, exactly? For a moment, this realization resurrected the hopelessness of her present situation.

CRACK! SQUEAK! WHOOMP! A door suddenly opened right in front of her, pouring bucketfuls of golden sunlight into her eyes.

Blinded AND frozen! Just Great.

Only momentarily this time, though. *That's improvement, at least,* she consoled herself, humorlessly.

Tilly peeked out through the opening, observing that she was among familiar tangled roots. She sniffed the air rushing towards her for telltale clues of danger. Her long bunny ears, sticking straight up now, rotated independently in all directions but failed to detect any foreboding sounds... so she simply stepped outside.

SLUMP! *YES!!* – She hadn't even jumped, having anticipated the portal's closing.

"Take that, Mr. Sneaky!"

CHAPTER 23

"*Ooh, now that really hurts, that does. Really. I get no respect. And to think of all I've done for you...*"

"Well, if you'd be nicer, maybe I would thank you more. I mean, shouldn't we at least know each other's proper names? Mine's Tilly. What's yours?"

"*Why, I'm Mr. Sneaky hadn't you heard?*"

"Ah, now come on. Don't be a Mr. Sour Puss, too! I just gave you that name because of what you said to me, and how you enjoyed scaring me at all the wrong times. I know you enjoyed it, so don't deny it. I could *feel* your happiness all the way down to my toes– each time I jumped."

"*Hah! I'll grant you that one, Bunny Girl!*"

"*Great sport, jumping jumpy Rabbits is*"

"I suppose that depends on one's perspective."

"Uhh, well... Harrump! Point taken! Let's get on with this 'adventure', shall we? Why do I agree to such things, anyway?" grumbled her invisible companion.

Tilly decided against asking more questions for the moment and generally looked around for the first time. She noted that the roots appeared strangely similar to the Old Elm's... Yet different, somehow.

She navigated her way through the tangled roots, her senses still on high alert for any danger. Something was wrong. Tilly didn't *feel* quite right, somehow. Lighter on her feet, perhaps?

Once outside the root maze, she turned her nose skyward, noting the Elm's large branches and alligator-skin bark. The tree's huge green leaves looked similar in shape to the Old Elm's, but they were far bigger and...

WOW! What was that!

Tilly had seen something larger than it should have been, flying past.

But that wasn't the real problem Tilly's mind was grappling with at that moment. Whatever had just flown by had been visible...*through* the leaves... They weren't green at all. They were clear as glass!

Which meant. Oh GEEZ! The sky must also be... Yep. GREEN as a toad's behind!

Something is definitely very wrong here. "Where, exactly am I?"

"THERE IT IS! The understatement of the Universe–HO HO HAH HEE, Ohh, HO HO HO!! Such brilliance! Such incisive insight. Stop it! HO HA HAHH– You're killing me here! YEE AH, AHAAH, HAAH, HA! "...Something's definitely very wrong here..." OOH, HARDY HAR HAR AH HAH AH-HAH! It's too much! OH, Stop it, PLEASE!!

"Would you, like, cut it out? I'm trying to think here and you're not helping at all," Tilly said too patiently. She obviously couldn't expect any help from Mr. Whoever-He-Was, so she'd need to investigate her immediate situation on her own.

She looked up again. Not only was the sky a deep emerald color, but hanging conspicuously right in the middle of it was a very large *Blue* moon! Yes, cobalt blue, with what appeared to be its own little moonlets zipping about, round-and-round, like beads on some unseen celestial string!

Just about that time, Tilly heard what must have been the strangest *sound* she'd ever encountered. Well, maybe not really a sound. More like a *feeling-sound,* actually. And it was literally *tapping* at her brain!

No. More precisely, *knocking.*

"Hello in there. Oh, won't you come out and talk to me? Open up in there. Oh, please!"

"Ahhh, Okay. What shall we talk about? Uh, I'm sorry. I didn't quite catch your name."

"That's all right. I don't really have one– just a 'picture-feeling'." Instantly a beautiful pale lavender butterfly appeared in Tilly's mind, with huge, strangely attractive, intelligent eyes and funny bottle-brush antennae... and then it began *fluttering* all around *inside* her brain!

She could feel its graceful wings, *tickling*! Yes, that was the correct way to describe it.

And she could *see* it, too, bumping into things, apologizing profusely and talking incessantly.

"I really can't tell you how excited I am to finally meet you! Oh, I just can't wait to show you around and see what you think of my– uhh– our world.

"We can discuss everything and play any game you want– forever, if you like."

"What exactly do you mean by, Forever?"

"Oh, you needn't worry about that just now. We have, Sooo much to do! We can talk all about that, whenever we have a free moment.

"Right now, let's take a flutter around so I can show you a few places where we might like to play together later.

"I can show you what flowers you can slurple. And those you really shouldn't, unless you want your wings to grow hairs; I mean, there's nothing wrong with having hair on your wings, mind you. It's just that they can sort of get in the way sometimes when you're trying to fly through straw

plants– One should never awaken the straw plants, you know. OH, there's so much to teach you!"

"But I can't fly. Really, it's not, well, a Rabbit sort of thing to do. We kind of prefer to stay on the ground. And, besides, I wouldn't know the first thing about flying."

Snicker. "Oh, sure you can!" her companion giggled. "Look. I don't really think you'll even need to try, actually?"

Tilly felt almost silly enough to entertain the idea– just for grins. She felt inexplicably giddy at the moment...*Strange, that.*

Something's truly gotten into me. Maybe it's in this air I'm breathing. I feel so... happy.

CHAPTER 24

For the first time since exiting the tree, Tilly looked down, noting her beautifully lithe, iridescent purple and orange wings fluttering gracefully all around her.

Her curiosity was briefly captured by the tiny bunny lying fast asleep upon a shiny elm root far below... The bunny looked somehow familiar? A distant acquaintance, perhaps? Yet, she couldn't quite place how she knew this, at that particular *moment* within which she now lived.